DOLPHINS SET II

CHINESE RIVER DOLPHINS

Kristin Petrie
ABDO Publishing Company

visit us at
www.abdopub.com

Published by ABDO Publishing Company, 4940 Viking Drive, Edina, Minnesota 55435.
Copyright © 2006 by Abdo Consulting Group, Inc. International copyrights reserved in all countries. No part of this book may be reproduced in any form without written permission from the publisher. The Checkerboard Library™ is a trademark and logo of ABDO Publishing Company.

Printed in the United States.

Cover Photo: © Roland Seitre / Seapics.com
Interior Photos: Animals Animals p. 21; Corbis pp. 10, 19; Getty Images p. 13; © Roland Seitre / Seapics.com p. 5; © Thomas Jefferson / Seapics.com pp. 15, 17; Uko Gorter pp. 6-7

Series Coordinator: Megan M. Gunderson
Editors: Heidi M. Dahmes, Megan M. Gunderson
Art Direction, Diagram, & Map: Neil Klinepier

Library of Congress Cataloging-in-Publication Data

Petrie, Kristin, 1970-
    Chinese river dolphins / Kristin Petrie.
        p. cm. -- (Dolphins. Set II)
    ISBN 1-59679-301-5
    1. Lipotes vexillifer--Juvenile literature. I. Title.

QL737.C436P482 2005
599.53'8--dc22

                                                    2005045799

CONTENTS

CHINESE RIVER DOLPHINS

The *Lipotes vexillifer* is the world's rarest dolphin. This dolphin is more commonly known as the Chinese river dolphin, or baiji. Like all dolphins, baiji are **cetaceans**. They are the only species in the **family** Lipotidae.

The Chinese river dolphin is a freshwater mammal. It calls China's Yangtze River home. The Yangtze is China's longest and most important river. Nearly one-third of China's population lives along the Yangtze. It is the only place where the baiji is found.

In the past, Chinese traditions protected this river dolphin. They believed one of their princesses was brought back to life as a baiji. The baiji has also been called the "Giant Panda of the Yangtze River." China's giant panda is an **endangered** species.

But today, the baiji are also threatened with extinction. No one knows for sure how many of them are left. But, scientists know the numbers are small.

Because Chinese river dolphins are separated from other dolphin species, the Greek word leipo was used for their scientific name. Leipo means "one who is left behind." The scientist who named this species used vexillifer, or "to bear a banner," for the second part of their name. He was told incorrectly that their Chinese name meant "flag bearer."

SIZE, SHAPE, AND COLOR

The Chinese river dolphin has a robust body. Male baiji weigh around 290 pounds (130 kg). And, they are more than seven feet (2 m) long. Female baiji tend to be slightly larger. They weigh around 370 pounds (170 kg). And, they are more than eight feet (2.5 m) long.

Chinese river dolphins have distinct features. They are recognized by their long, slightly up-turned snout.

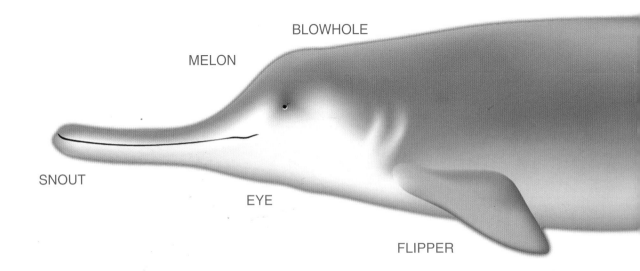

BLOWHOLE

MELON

SNOUT

EYE

FLIPPER

Their mouth line curves up near the corners. It looks like these dolphins are smiling! Their tiny eyes are set high on the forehead.

Chinese river dolphins have a blunt-tipped, triangular **dorsal** fin and an oval-shaped blowhole. They also have puffy cheeks and a rounded **melon**. Like some other river dolphins, baiji have a **flexible** neck. This allows them to navigate the river more easily.

Chinese river dolphins are gray with a white belly. The white and gray pattern near the head looks like brushstrokes. This pattern is different on each dolphin. So, sometimes individual baiji can be identified by their coloring.

DORSAL FIN

FLUKE

WHERE THEY LIVE

The Chinese river dolphin is a freshwater mammal. This species was once found in several freshwater rivers and lakes. Other than the Yangtze, these included China's Qiangtang and Fuchun rivers. They also lived in the Dongting and Poyang lakes of China.

Many years ago, the rivers and lakes were clean and unobstructed. But over time, human-made dams were constructed. These dams prevented dolphins and other river life from spreading out into their usual **habitats**.

Today, the few remaining baiji are found only in the main part of the Yangtze River. They like to live in river confluences. This is where rivers or channels come together. Baiji also like areas around islands and sandbars.

But, the Chinese river dolphin is in danger of disappearing from the Yangtze altogether. The river has become polluted. And, it is overrun with boats. These things put the Chinese river dolphin in danger of extinction.

Arctic Ocean

NORTH AMERICA

EUROPE

ASIA

Atlantic Ocean

AFRICA

Pacific Ocean

Pacific Ocean

SOUTH AMERICA

Indian Ocean

AUSTRALIA

N

Where Chinese River Dolphins Live

Pacific Ocean

Yangtze River

CHINA

SENSES

Chinese river dolphins have poor eyesight. Luckily, the baiji's other senses are much stronger. These dolphins rely more on their sense of hearing when their **habitat** is muddy or polluted. And, they rely on something called echolocation.

Echolocation turns sound into information. To use echolocation, a dolphin makes noises that travel through the water. These sounds bounce off land, river life, and other objects. Then, these sounds return to the dolphin.

Even in clear tropical waters, many ocean dolphins rely on echolocation.

The sounds that return tell the dolphin the size and the distance of an object. Baiji use this information to figure out their location. Echolocation is also used to find food. And, it helps the dolphins avoid danger.

Sound wave sent out by dolphin

Echo wave received by dolphin

DEFENSE

Some dolphin species have natural **predators**, such as killer whales or sharks. Chinese river dolphins have a different type of threat. Their threat comes from humans.

Human-made dams keep dolphins from their natural homes and breeding areas. These dams also reduce the number of fish available for the dolphins to eat.

Pollution from industries along the river affects the quality of their **habitat**. Fishers and boat propellers are also threats. They accidentally injure and kill river life, including baiji and their prey.

These human problems have dramatically harmed the population size of Chinese river dolphins. The dolphins have no defense against these threats. So, there may be fewer than 100 individuals left! For this reason, baiji are considered a critically **endangered** mammal.

Some people are trying to defend this species against the human threat. In one area, a council spreads information about the dolphins and about what can be done to protect them. Other organizations are trying to relocate the dolphins to safer **environments**.

Finless porpoises also live in the Yangtze River. They are threatened by pollution and habitat destruction, too.

FOOD

Chinese river dolphins tend to live in deeper areas of the Yangtze River. However, they often swim to shallower waters for feeding. There, they feed on small river fish. Echolocation helps them locate their prey.

Chinese river dolphins also dive to the river bottom for food. Usually, their dives last about 10 to 20 seconds. They use their long beaks to stir up the mud and snacks!

Baiji eat their prey head first. Scientists believe this helps them eat the fish safely. This way, the prey's sharp spines do not get caught in the dolphin's throat.

Opposite page: *Chinese river dolphins are strong swimmers and can travel great distances. Scientists tracked three dolphins who traveled 60 miles (97 km) in just three days!*

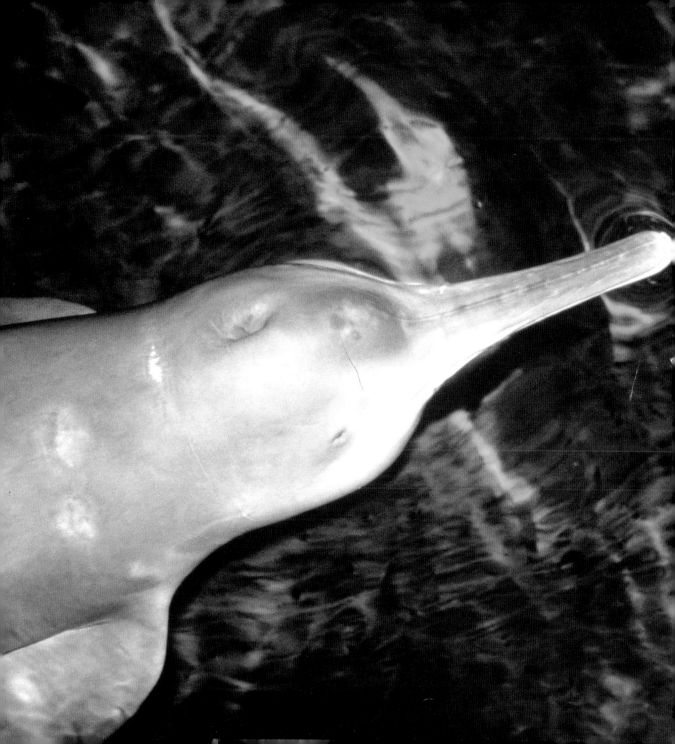

BABIES

Little is known about the reproduction of Chinese river dolphins. Scientists believe the male dolphins mature around four years of age. It is believed the females mature sometime after age six. Mating usually takes place in April or May.

A Chinese river dolphin is probably **pregnant** for 10 to 11 months. Baiji give birth between February and March. One baby dolphin is born at a time. A baby dolphin is called a calf. Like other mammals, calves are nursed with their mother's milk after birth.

Mother baiji and their babies seem to have a strong bond. But eventually, the calf is **weaned** and must feed itself. Mothers have one calf about once every two years. No one knows for sure how long the rare Chinese river dolphin lives, but some estimate about 24 years.

The only baiji China had in captivity died in 2002. He was named Qi Qi. Scientists had hoped Qi Qi could help them increase the number of baiji left. Relocation of another captured baiji was unsuccessful.

BEHAVIORS

Chinese river dolphins are one of the world's rarest mammals. They are the most **endangered cetacean**. Still, not much is known about this species. Baiji are shy and avoid boats. This makes them difficult to observe.

In their natural **habitat**, baiji are most often seen in **pods** of two to six. They have also been observed in larger pods of up to 16 dolphins. However, it has been many years since scientists have seen pods of more than ten baiji.

Chinese river dolphins have also been known to travel long distances. But with dam construction and other habitat loss, travel becomes more difficult. Scientists worry that the Chinese river dolphin may soon become extinct.

Opposite page: *When completed, the Three Gorges Dam will be the largest in the world. It will provide flood protection and electricity for millions of people. But, it adds to the habitat destruction of the Chinese river dolphin.*

CHINESE RIVER DOLPHIN FACTS

Scientific Name: *Lipotes vexillifer*

Common Names: Chinese River Dolphin, Yangtze River Dolphin, Baiji, White Fin Dolphin, White Flag Dolphin

Average Size: Females weigh about 370 pounds (170 kg). On average, they are more than 8 feet (2.5 m) long. Males typically weigh about 290 pounds (130 kg) and are more than 7 feet (2 m) long.

Where They're Found: Yangtze River in China

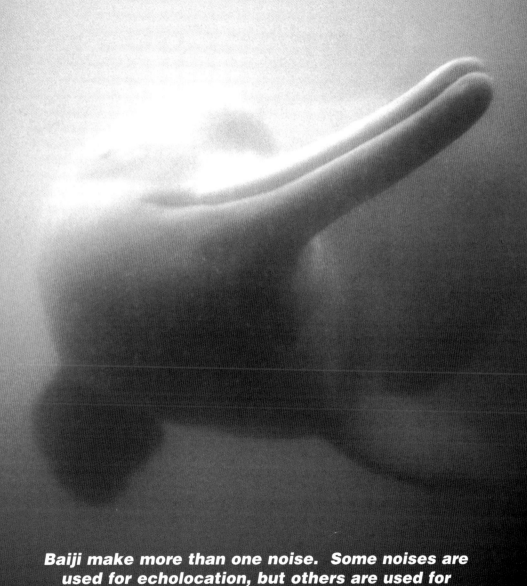

Baiji make more than one noise. Some noises are used for echolocation, but others are used for communication. And sometimes, they make a high-pitched sneezing sound when they surface to breathe.

GLOSSARY

cetacean (sih-TAY-shuhn) - any of various types of mammal, such as the dolphin, that live in water like fish.

dorsal - located near or on the back, especially of an animal.

endangered - in danger of becoming extinct.

environment - all the surroundings that affect the growth and well-being of a living thing.

family - a group that scientists use to classify similar plants or animals. It ranks above a genus and below an order.

flexible - able to bend or move easily.

habitat - a place where a living thing is naturally found.

melon - the rounded forehead of some cetaceans, which may aid in echolocation.

pod - a group of animals, typically whales or dolphins.

predator - an animal that kills and eats other animals.

pregnant - having one or more babies growing within the body.

wean - to accustom an animal to eat food other than its mother's milk.

WEB SITES

To learn more about Chinese river dolphins, visit ABDO Publishing Company on the World Wide Web at **www.abdopub.com**. Web sites about these dolphins are featured on our Book Links page. These links are routinely monitored and updated to provide the most current information available.

INDEX

24